Written by: Jessica Ward
Illustrations by: Monty Maldovan
Renderings by: Robert Vann
Designed by: Winnie Ho

Printed in Malaysia
First Edition
10 9 8 7 6 5 4 3 2
ISBN 978-1-4231-4585-1
Visit www.disneybooks.com
H106-9333-5-12268

Duffy
The Disney Bear
Mickey's New Friend

 PRESS
New York

Mickey is a sea captain, so naturally, he spends a lot of time on the ocean. But sometimes he gets lonely being away from Minnie for so long.

Minnie has a seaside workshop where she makes all sort of crafts. One day she had an idea.

She decided to make Mickey
a teddy bear to keep him
company on his long voyages.

As she sewed, she thought about the fun
adventures that she and Mickey had had
together, and she filled the bear
with happy memories and love.

When it was time for Mickey to set out
on his next trip, Minnie went with him to
the pier. She handed him a small duffel bag.
When Mickey opened it, he discovered the
adorable stuffed bear that Minnie had made
for him. Mickey was overjoyed.

"This is the best going-away gift ever!" Mickey exclaimed, and he gave Minnie a hug.

"You can keep him in your duffel and take him with you wherever you go," she replied.

"I will! And I think I will name him Duffy," Mickey declared.

The next day was a busy one. Mickey had a crew of new sailors to train, and he hardly had a moment to rest. But after dinner, Mickey went down into his cabin and began to feel homesick. He missed Minnie, so he picked up Duffy and hugged him tight.

As Mickey squeezed the little bear, a magical feeling came over him. All of a sudden, he felt the love that Minnie had sewed into Duffy, and he wasn't homesick anymore. He curled up in his bunk and fell asleep holding the bear close to his heart.

Love,
MINNIE

That night, Mickey had a dream. He dreamed that Duffy came alive and spoke to him. And this is what the little bear said: "Mickey, whenever you start to miss home, all you have to do is give me a hug and the love that Minnie put inside of me will chase away your sadness."

In the morning when
Mickey woke up, he looked
down at Duffy and smiled.
To this day, Mickey still
swears that the teddy bear
smiled back at him
and winked.

After that, Mickey and Duffy were inseparable. Together they traveled all over the world and visited many new and exciting places. And of course they made lots of friends along the way.

They trekked through
a jungle, rode a camel
across a desert, and tried
all different sorts of food
(well Mickey did, anyway).
Everywhere they went,
Mickey and Duffy took
pictures.

When Mickey got home, he told Minnie and his friends about all his adventures with Duffy. He told them about the dream he had about Duffy coming to life. Then he showed them all the pictures he had taken, and everyone knew Duffy was one special little bear.

It wasn't long before Mickey's friends began asking Minnie if they could have Duffys, too. They all wanted travel teddies who would make them feel loved and keep them company during their journeys.

At first it was difficult for Minnie to keep up
with all her friends' requests. But she was
a very smart mouse, and she quickly
transformed her workshop
into Duffy-making central.

Once Minnie's friends had Duffys of their own, they set off on trips with their little stuffed sidekicks.

Pretty soon they began
sending Minnie pictures
of themselves posing
with their Duffys in
locations far and wide.

Now that you have your very own Duffy to travel with, you can hug him whenever you feel lonely and take pictures with him to send back to your friends. Where will you and Duffy go next?